MAUDIE'S UMBRELLA

MAUDIE'S UMBRELLA

written and illustrated by KAY CHORAO

E. P. DUTTON & CO., INC.   NEW YORK

Text and illustrations copyright © 1975 by Kay Sproat Chorao

All rights reserved. No part of this publication may be
reproduced or transmitted in any form or by any means,
electronic or mechanical, including photocopy, recording,
or any information storage and retrieval system now
known or to be invented, without permission in writing
from the publisher, except by a reviewer who wishes to
quote brief passages in connection with a review written
for inclusion in a magazine, newspaper, or broadcast.

Library of Congress Cataloging in Publication Data

Chorao, Kay Sproat   Maudie's umbrella

SUMMARY: Maudie can't find the umbrella she'd decorated
with E's for Queen Emily. Then she runs into her friend Elsie.

[1. Friendship—Fiction]   I. Title.
PZ7.C4463Mau   [E]   75-5922   ISBN 0-525-34770-4

Published simultaneously in Canada by Clarke,
Irwin & Company Limited, Toronto and Vancouver

Designed by Riki Levinson
Printed in the U.S.A.   First Edition
10 9 8 7 6 5 4 3 2 1

For JAMIE,
who keeps losing the mouthpiece
to his trumpet

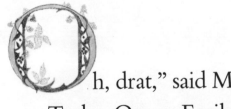"h, drat," said Maudie. "I need eyeglasses."
Today Queen Emily would be crowned.
Everyone would bring a present for her.
"I traded my best handmade bean pot for that
gold umbrella. And I hurt my eyes sewing on
all those fancy E's."
But the umbrella was nowhere to be seen.

So Maudie grabbed a crocodile cookie jar instead.
"After all, a handmade cookie jar by Maudie Mole
is nothing to sniff at."

She ran through the raspberry patch
and rang for her best friend, Elsie.
But Elsie had already left.
So Maudie scampered on her way.

Just at the edge of the woods, something
caught Maudie's eye.
"My lost umbrella!"
She ran up to a curved handle, half hidden
in some baby ferns.

She gave the handle a YANK!

"Oh, I beg your pardon, Edgar," said Maudie.
"I thought your tail was my umbrella."
"Next time wear your specs," grumbled Edgar.

"Oh dear," said Maudie, picking her way
through some dead leaves. "But wait!"

Maudie saw something round and gold behind
an old log. Could it be what she thought it was?

She peeped over the log.

"Shhhhhhhh," whispered Pablo Bear.

"I'm watching an ant carry a raisin."

"Oh. I thought your pants were my umbrella,"
whispered Maudie.

"They're just pants," whispered Pablo.

"Oh," whispered Maudie. "Bye."
"Bye," whispered Pablo.
He watched Maudie hurry away.

She spied something round
         and gold
            and glittery.

"Help," yelled Maudie.

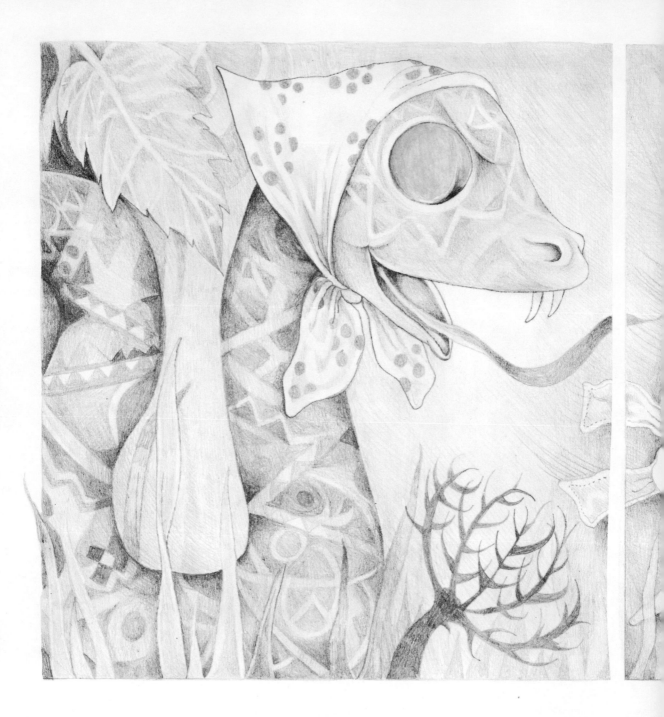

"Help, help, HELP!"
She ran and stumbled and ran.

It could have been the end of Maudie.
But Sally Snake saw a juicy mouse and
lost interest in moles.

So, tired but safe, Maudie arrived at
the coronation grounds.
Some children giggled when Maudie
put her present on the table.

And when Maudie tried to see Queen Emily
get her crown, all she could see were the backs
of heads, <u>and</u>

her best friend, Elsie, holding *Maudie's Umbrella!*

"Oh, Maudie, thank you for my beautiful birthday
umbrella with E's for Elsie on it. What fun it was
to find a birthday present in our raspberry patch."
Of course, thought Maudie, I used it one very
hot day when I was gathering berries for lunch.
"I'm so happy you like it," said Maudie.

And the next day Maudie gave a party for Elsie.

It was more fun than a coronation.

KAY CHORAO is the author-illustrator of a number of picture books, including *Ralph and the Queen's Bathtub* (Farrar, Straus & Giroux). Her illustrations have appeared in two Dutton titles by Barbara Williams, *Kevin's Grandma* and *Albert's Toothache*. The latter was an ALA Notable Children's Book of 1974, as well as a selection of the Children's Book Showcase and the American Institute of Graphic Arts Fifty Books Show.

Kay Chorao says her acquaintance with moles dates back to when she was in fourth grade in a tiny country school, where a mole was found during recess. It left a place in her affections, and although "Maudie is not a realistic mole (her eyes are too big, her front paws too small), she expressed my vision of moleness."

Ms. Chorao lives in New York City with her husband, a painter, and their three children.

The display type for the title was set in Cicero and the other display and text in Griffo. The art was drawn in soft pencil with a color overlay in pencil as well. The book was printed by offset at Halliday Lithographers.